Franklin's School Play

For Rachel – PB

For Sandi, who was born
to perform – BC

ISBN 0-590-69331-X

Text copyright © 1996 by Paulette Bourgeois
Illustrations copyright © 1996 by Brenda Clark
FRANKLIN and the FRANKLIN character are trademarks of
Kids Can Press Ltd.
All rights reserved. Published by Scholastic Inc., 555 Broadway, New York,
NY 10012, by arrangement with Kids Can Press Ltd.
Interior illustrations prepared with the assistance of Shelley Southern.

12 11 10 9 8 7 6 5 4 3 2 1   6 7 8 9/9 0 1/0

Printed in the U.S.A.   23

First Scholastic printing, November 1996

Franklin's School Play

Paulette Bourgeois
Brenda Clark

SCHOLASTIC INC.

New York   Toronto   London   Auckland   Sydney

FRANKLIN could count forwards and backwards. He could remember his phone number, his address, and the names of six different shapes. But sometimes Franklin was forgetful. So he worried when Mr. Owl chose him to play one of the lead roles in the class play. What if he forgot his lines?

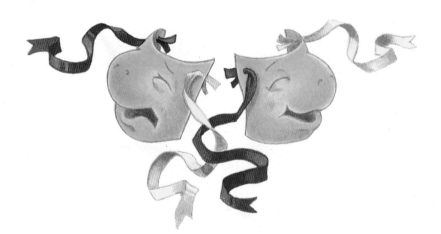

Every December, Mr. Owl's students put on a show that they made up themselves. This year they would perform *A Salute to the Nutcracker.*

Franklin had seen the *Nutcracker* ballet with his parents, and he'd listened to the music at home. He loved the story about a little girl and the toy soldier who comes to life.

Franklin had a big part to learn. At home he said his lines over and over again.

"I hope I don't forget what to say," he told his parents.

They encouraged him. "If you practice, you'll be fine."

Franklin wasn't so sure.

The week before the show, there was a flurry of activity in the classroom.

Everyone had an important job to do.

Goose studied her lines. Beaver practiced her ballet steps. The musicians learned their songs.

"Lovely! Lovely!" said Mr. Owl.

Raccoon was in charge of building the sets. His team had already cut, glued, painted, and decorated most of the scenery. Now they were busy trimming the tree. Mr. Owl thought it was spectacular.

Bear was the costume designer. He and his friends created wonderful costumes with bits of this and that.

When Mr. Owl saw what they had made, he clapped and said, "Delightful!"

The cast practiced speaking loudly and clearly.
Badger was the stage manager, so she prompted the
players when they couldn't remember their lines.
   "That's great," said Mr. Owl. "But where is Franklin?"
Raccoon pointed to the art supply cupboard.

Franklin peeked out. "I need a quiet place to learn my lines," he said. "I get to the middle and then I forget."

"Let's work on them together," suggested Mr. Owl.

By the end of the day, Franklin could say his lines without missing a word.

"Bravo!" said Mr. Owl.

It was the day before the show. The programs were printed, and the seats were set up. For the first time, the students would practice onstage. Mr. Owl directed everyone to their places.

Rabbit thumped his feet in excitement.

"Quiet, please," said Mr. Owl. "Curtain time."

Franklin went over the lines in his head.

The curtain opened. Franklin was silent.
Mr. Owl whispered, "It's time to begin."
Franklin tried to talk, but his throat was
tight. Every time he looked at the empty seats,
he was scared.

"Psst," said Badger. "I'll tell you what to say."

But Franklin didn't need a prompter. He
remembered the lines. He just couldn't say
them out loud.

Mr. Owl talked to Franklin alone.

"Maybe you have stage fright," said Mr. Owl.
"Try not to think about the audience."

Franklin tried three more times. But each time
the curtain opened, Franklin's mouth stayed closed.

He didn't want to give up, but they were
running out of time. So Franklin asked Mr. Owl if
he could switch places with Badger. She could
play the Nutcracker Prince because she knew all
the lines.

They started again. Badger couldn't be heard at the back of the room.

Mr. Owl nudged Franklin. "Why don't you help her out."

Franklin stood onstage beside Badger. "Try saying your lines like this."

Franklin spoke in a booming voice. He meant to say just one line. But Franklin got carried away and said a whole speech.

When he was finished, everyone cheered.

"You got over your stage fright!" said Mr. Owl.

"I guess I did," laughed Franklin.

Badger looked relieved.

The next night, when the curtain opened,
Franklin saw his family sitting in the front row.
He took a deep breath.

Franklin's first words were soft and raspy.
Keep going, he told himself. And he did. Franklin
acted so well that he almost believed he really
was the Nutcracker Prince.

It was a marvelous show. After the finale,
the audience gave the class a standing ovation.
Franklin and his friends bowed four times.

And that night, after a hot cocoa by the fire,
Franklin pasted the show program into his scrapbook.
It was a night he wanted to remember forever.